Cooper's Story

Cooper's Story

Holly R. Bohling

Bohling, Inc.

Bohling Inc.

Bohling, Holly

ISBN 978-1-7333788-8-8

Cover Design by Holly R. Bohling

Book Design by Holly R. Bohling

Dedication

This book is dedicated to all the pets we love. When you come home to the joyful warmth of a dog's love, the outside world fades away as you share greetings. Their unconditional love for us, patience, loyalty, and dedication make all the difference in our daily lives.

Table of Contents

Prologue

The heartfelt compassion animal lovers demonstrate for the animal kingdom in distress is awe inspiring. Their work is never done. They can only help one life at a time, but for that one life, it makes all the difference. Informal rescue workers are everywhere. We have neighbors down the street who are known to be our local cat rescue team, we know to take a lost kitty to them. Others work with dogs, birds, turtles and more. Thankfully, some become actively involved as formal volunteers assisting organizations caring for lost and distressed animals. Many choose animal rescue as a profession, making a career of working in this field. From city streets, small towns, the wilderness and forests, their work is unending.

According to the World Health Organization, there are around 200 million stray dogs across the globe. North America has over 70 million stray dogs. According to petpedia.co 1.5 million animals are euthanized in shelters each year. [i]

Only one in ten dogs will have a permanent home. Three thousand five hundred animal shelters in the U.S., annually shelter 6-8 million cats and dogs. The primary reasons: being born on the street or owner abandonment.

Michael Broad, former attorney and animal lover from the United Kingdom describes the community that supports these animals as: "The sort of people who work in animal rescue are going to be sensitive, decent and kind people. They are going to be the kind of people who care by which I mean genuinely care about the welfare of animals."[ii]

The situation is dire, and the job of caring for these animals is overwhelming and unending. Sometimes animal workers, techs, veterinarians, and animal rescue volunteers experience 'compassion fatigue.'

Jessica Dolce, a Certified Compassion Fatigue Educator, says, "Compassion fatigue is an occupational hazard of our work with animals, whether you are an animal control officer or kennel attendant in a small town or an internationally recognized veterinarian. Our work requires that we compassionately and effectively respond to the constant demand to be helping those who are suffering and in need." [iii]

This novel is just one story among millions, where informal and formal resources come together to help a stray dog in need. Again, one life at a time, each animal helped by these folks makes all the difference in that animal's life.

Holly R. Bohling

Chapter 1

Wolf!

"Ben! I'm glad you answered! There is a white wolf outside!" Jenny cried as she hollered into the phone. Her husband, on the other end, was stunned.

"Get the kids and stay inside!" Ben said sternly, "Then call the humane society!"

"He's walking funny! Like a stealth thing!" she went on as she stood at the window and watched the animal walk away. "Maybe he has rabies!" she paused. "He's past us now. That was weird!"

That evening she posted her story on the local online neighborhood news feed. People started responding:

"I saw it a week ago. Is it a wolf?"

"It's not a wolf, it's a white dog!"

"But it looked at me. Its eyes are yellow!!"

"We don't have wolves. It must be a coyote! What color is it?"

"White and gray with a long shaggy tail."

"Sounds like a coyote to me."

"No, people, it's a shepherd-husky mix. The local rescue group is trying to catch it. Contact them and give them your address so they can set a humane trap."

"I think it's a wolf!"

"It's part shepherd and husky. They look like that. Don't worry it's NOT a wolf."

"Well, somebody better get that animal off the streets! It's not safe for our children and pets."

After a couple days, the comments faded, and no one saw the animal for a while.

Chapter 2

Tucker

Three months earlier:

"Good boy, Tucker!" Robert praised his puppy and gave him a treat. "Karen, this fella is smart! He learns with just a couple tries." Inside the house Karen heard Robert through the window screen. She smiled as she washed dishes and watched her husband with his dog. She had not wanted another dog, but her husband, Robert, loved animals, particularly dogs. They had dogs ever since they married. But now, after 55 years together, she felt they shouldn't have any more pets, especially big dogs.

"What will happen, Robert, if we suddenly can't take care of him?" Karen had asked when he first brought the white shepherd-husky mix home to meet her.

"Karen, I've spent my whole life with dogs, training and caring for them. I have to have one." Robert told her. "I will make sure it is a gentle dog."

Robert showed up with the puppy. "Here he is Karen, he's a great puppy. Smart, curious, and very gentle. See?" Robert reached out to the dog with a tiny treat between his fingers, and the white pup gently nibbled at the treat, waiting for Robert to release it. Karen agreed he was gentle, but she still felt it was too much to have a big dog. The days passed, and Robert spent hours with Tucker.

"It looks like a shepherd but also like a husky. What breed is it?" Karen asked.

Robert answered, "It's a husky-shepherd mix. The breeder has been breeding this combination for years. They make very healthy, smart, gentle dogs. But they are also protectors that know the rules and expect everyone to follow them."

"I see," answered Karen, "It's still a puppy, how much bigger will he get?"

"I expect he will grow to be about 80 to 90 pounds." Then, changing the subject, Robert went on, "But isn't he beautiful? He is so white; he glows in the dark! He was the only white puppy they had."

Karen began to warm up as she looked into the dog's eyes, "Oh my! And his eyes are so golden, and it looks like he is wearing eyeliner!" She smiled. "Even his golden eyes look gentle."

Robert thought to himself and smiled, "I believe he has won her heart." Then aloud, he said, "Well, honey, we need to name him. I was thinking of calling him Tucker. What do you think, Karen?"

"Honey, he's your dog, you name him. Tucker works for me." Karen responded.

Weeks passed, and during this time, Robert trained Tucker to sit, stay and come. The dog quickly learned to go potty outside. Using the doggie door, he could go out independently as needed. In fact, he took his business far away from where the family spent time together on the patio in the evenings. In the evenings he sat apart from Robert and Karen as they sat on their back patio. "It's almost as if he is watching over us." Robert commented. Tucker always kept Robert in his line of vision. The two were together most of the time.

One evening, Robert came in from working with Tucker, "Karen, I'm going to have the neighbors come over with their two dogs to play. Tucker needs those big dogs for exercise. I can't wear him out myself here in the yard, and it's too hot to take him hiking. Their dogs wore him out last time they came over. Your little Frisky can't do it."

Frisky was Karen's dog, a 12-year-old chihuahua. Frisky used to be frisky, but now he just wanted to lie around and sleep. With Tucker there, Frisky stayed on the couch, out of the big puppy's way. Tucker was a playful dog, growing quickly, and did not yet realize he was much stronger than Frisky.

Robert couldn't run and hike with him like he had done with his earlier dogs, so he played fetch with him in the back yard to be sure he burned off his energy. Tucker's favorite toy was a large squeaky pig. Robert threw it as far as he could, and Tucker ran full throttle to snatch it up and then he kept on running. The puppy loved to toss it in the air and leap up to catch it as it fell to the ground.

When Tucker was about 16 months old, he learned a new command on his own. Robert was surprised when it happened. It must have been something he'd been doing when he taught Tucker to come. It was a warm afternoon, and Robert had been running and playing fetch with Tucker. Robert was trying to take it easy, but it was such fun. Karen watched from the kitchen window as she cleaned the supper dishes. Robert was sweating and Tucker was panting. The two were having a great time, but both were quite hot. "Robert, I think you two better to come back in. It's hot out there."

"Sure, in a minute." He was out of breath and sounded excited, "But Karen! First, you've gotta see this!" Robert cried out from the yard, interrupting her thoughts. "Watch!"

The couple had an acreage, and the back yard was huge, allowing the white husky mix to run and play with all his might. "See? He's over there in the north corner. Watch him come running when I do this!" Robert stood straight and tall, silently reaching his arm full length and pointed in the air toward the pup. The minute Tucker saw Robert's arm in the air, he came running full speed back to his master, carrying his favorite bone in his mouth. Tucker dropped the bone at Robert's feet and the two greeted each other with joy.

Tucker loved pleasing his master. Karen smiled and was glad to see both so happy. Karen smiled to herself, accepting her fate. "Robert is happy with his dogs," she thought. "I can't keep him from his greatest joy."

"Good dog!" Robert said, picked up the bone, and threw Tucker's toy back out to the north corner. Tucker ran off to capture the toy as Karen looked back down to finish the dishes. In just that moment, she heard a grunt, a thud, and silence. She looked up from the dishes and saw Robert lying on the ground. Tucker was in the far corner of the yard and, also, looked up at the odd sounds. Dropping her dish, she ran out to her husband. Standing in the far corner of the yard, Tucker did the same thing, dropping his toy he ran back to Robert, sensing something was wrong.

Karen and Tucker met at Robert's lifeless body. "No!" cried Karen. She shook him and there was no response. "No!" She cried again. Tucker whined and pawed at Robert's shoulder as if trying to help Karen. Karen ran back into the house to grab her phone and called 911.

The 911 operator was giving Karen instructions for CPR when the paramedics arrived through the side yard gate. Karen looked up and sighed with relief, hoping they could bring him back to life. She stood and stepped back as the paramedics kneeled next to Robert. Tucker continued to lay nearby and did not bark at the paramedics, sensing their presence was necessary.

The next day she was surrounded by their three children. Karen was sitting on her recliner crying. Her eldest daughter, Emily, sat beside her trying to console her mother, "Mom, he had a good life. There was nothing you could do." She paused for her mother to respond. Karen kept crying. Emily went on, "His heart attack was so massive, the doctor said even if he'd been in the hospital when it happened, they couldn't have started it again!"

Bob, her eldest and the practical one, stood beside them, "Mom, we need to make plans. First, we need to plan his funeral and then we need to decide where you are going to live. This place is just too big for you!" Karen looked at her son for a moment and buried her face in her hands.

It was too much to deal with right now. She loved Robert. They had been high school sweethearts and married right after graduation. She worked while he went to college and received his degree in architecture. He'd had a scholarship but still, those early years were difficult. But they loved being poor, together. Oscar was their puppy then. He was a little Boston Terrier, and it wasn't too expensive to feed Oscar. Now, she was alone, and she missed him so very much.

"And Mom, let me take Tucker off your hands. He can come to our home with the kids, and we will find a new home for him."

Karen hadn't thought of how she would handle Tucker, "Thank you Bob, I almost forgot to feed him this morning!" She felt badly about that. "When I came home from the hospital, he was so sweet, waiting beside the pantry, hoping I would get his food for him. He made me remember to feed him. He is a good dog."

Tucker lay quietly at her feet chewing on his favorite bone. She looked at him remembering how much Robert loved this dog. It would be hard to lose him too, but she knew she couldn't handle him by herself. "I think he understands." Karen said to her family. "Dogs sense things like this." She hesitated for a moment to gather her thoughts, "Let me keep him a little longer. Maybe after the funeral. I can't take too much more change right now." The kids stood in a semicircle around their mother and watched Tucker as he chewed his bone.

The following days and weeks were a blur to Karen. After the funeral, she was ready to begin thinking about her future. The children took turns checking in on her once a week. After a month, Bob stopped by to visit and asked Karen how Tucker was doing. He wanted to explain that his wife did not want to keep Tucker. "You know Mom, Jen doesn't want him. He's too big for our house. We don't have space or the yard for him. But I've checked around and know someone who said he could take him."

Karen smiled, "Okay, I understand. It's time," she hesitated a moment thinking about letting Tucker go, then went on, "Thanks, Bob. Be sure to get his dog food; there is a huge bag in there. It's so big, I can't even pick it up."

The following Saturday, Bob took Tucker to his friend's house. "Hi Curt, here he is."

"He is one mighty handsome boy!" Curt exclaimed. "You said he is good with kids?"

"Yes, he is gentle and smart." Bob responded. "If he gets enough exercise, he's perfect. He wants to follow the rules. Once he knows them, Tucker will be a good boy; and he is happy when he learns a new trick."

"Got it," Curt responded as he took the leash. Bob went to his car and came back with a giant bag of dog food, a dog bed, and a dish.

"You can have these."

"Great, thanks." Once unloaded, Bob turned away and got back in his car and drove off while Tucker watched him drive away. This would not be the only time Tucker watched a car leave him behind.

Curt turned around and headed into the house. He and his wife had talked about getting a dog, so when Bob mentioned

Tucker, Curt thought it would be a perfect fit. He unhooked the leash as they entered the house, and his two boys squealed with delight when they saw Tucker. "Yay! A puppy!" They cried, running up to the dog. Tucker picked up on the boys' energy and began dashing about the house, leaping onto the living room furniture. The picture behind the couch came tumbling down behind Tucker. Startled, Tucker leaped off the couch, ran from the living room to the kitchen, knocking over the table lamp. When he tried to spin back toward the living room, he skidded in a circle as he maneuvered.

The boys ran for cover, squealing and laughing. Jill, their mother, clasped her mouth and screamed to see the big white puppy dash through the house. Curt burst out laughing thoroughly enjoying the moment.

"Stop him!" Jill cried. Curt stopped laughing and tried to catch Tucker as he dashed past him a third time. The dog whizzed past. On Tucker's fourth time around, Curt was able to grab him by wrapping his arms around the dog's neck. The two fell on the floor and slid across the kitchen floor, both breathing heavily. Curt laughed again, thoroughly enjoying the chaos. But Jill was white with emotion and yelled, "He knocked over the lamp!"

Curt and Tucker continue to lay on the floor as things quieted down. The wide-eyed boys slowly walked out from behind the bedroom doors, peeking around the corner to be sure all was safe. Tucker had settled down, panting as he lay on the kitchen floor with

Curt by his side. "We need to talk about whether this dog can stay," Jill said. "We will talk tonight after dinner."

"But Mom!" both boys cried together. "He's perfect!" Tucker had settled down and let the boys crawl on him and tickle his tummy. The boys and Tucker played together all evening. After the boys had gone to bed, Jill came down the steps and promptly sat down next to Curt and started talking, "Curt, we can't keep this dog. He's too big for us."

Curt already knew this was coming. Looking at the dog, sleeping on the floor, "But he's good now; it was just a crazy beginning!" He protested weakly. Jill looked at him sternly and he didn't argue anymore. He realized she was not going to budge, and he must figure out what to do with the new dog.

She went on, "And did you see the price tag on his dog food bag; it's almost $50! We can't afford that! And did you notice he hasn't been fixed yet? Who knows what that will cost?"

"I don't know, Jill," Curt said quietly, still considering what to do with Tucker. "I don't know what to do with him. I can't give him back to Bob."

"Well, let me figure it out. I can call around tomorrow morning."

The following day at breakfast, Jill explained to the boys that Tucker was not going to stay. "Boys, Tucker is just too big and expensive for us." Jill went on, "So I will take him to find another home today."

Curt watched the boys' reaction as he stood by Tucker, petting his ears. "Hey, guys, we will get a another, smaller dog, I promise. It just can't be this one.

Chapter 3

Alone

Tucker sat on the sidewalk as he watched the blue car and the blonde lady drive away. The car disappeared, and Tucker sat down, whined, and waited for the car to return. After a while he lay down, keeping his eyes facing the direction the car had taken. But it didn't come back.

Eventually, he looked around feeling very alone. He was in a different place. Nothing looked familiar. He thought of Robert and somehow, he knew Robert would not be coming for him. Robert wasn't the same anymore. The dog slowly laid his head back down, thinking it would be best to wait a while. He closed his eyes for a short nap, still expecting someone would come and get him. It was late morning, and he generally took a nap about this time of day, anyway.

Soon, the heat of the sun awakened him. It was a hot desert afternoon. He sat and stretched, out his hind legs, enjoying the feel of his muscles as they stretched. He yawned a noisy yawn as he usually does when waking up from a nap. Only this time, Robert wasn't there to give him a wake-up hug. Looking around, he saw a field of green grass and wandered that direction, sitting down in the shade under a tree. It was cool and refreshing as his stomach gurgled, reminding him it was dinner time. Tucker watched across the grass and noticed people walking around with sticks and hitting balls into tiny holes in the grass. Tucker didn't know this, but it was a golf course. He stood there for a moment and decided to walk, following the smell of water which led him toward the pond.

The golfers watched the beautiful white pup walk by as if it knew where it was going. One of the golfers was overheard, saying "Interesting dog, that its owners let it wander the golf course like that."

At the pond, he noticed ducks and plenty of birds surrounding the water. The fowl flew away with Tucker's approach. Instinctively, he joyfully jumped forward toward the closest bird as it fluttered away.

He took a drink of water from the pond and lay down again near the pond. "Maybe someone will bring food." He had not yet given up on that idea. But shortly, he would realize, no one would be coming. The sun went down, and dark set in. The last of the golfers watched Tucker lying on the grass as he fell asleep. He had not yet learned to hide.

Soon he would be the talk of the neighborhood.

Tucker heard all kinds of sounds during the night. An owl hooting and coyotes, yelping in the distance. He listened to the rustling of the ringtail cats in the trees. All of these were new sounds for a young pup who'd spent his nights in the house. His ears were perked and alert the whole night. He didn't sleep well; each new sound aroused him from his sleep, and he listened carefully to figure out what caused the noises. His nose worked double-time as he tried to localize the scent and match it to the sounds.

The following morning, Tucker woke up with the sound of a mockingbird. He'd heard those before and knew those were the things that would fly in the air. Soon birds were flying and hopping along the ground, searching for seeds and bugs. Again, his stomach reminded him he hadn't eaten last night, and now it was time for breakfast. In addition, he noticed how thirsty he'd gotten. He smelled the pond water and headed back over to it. Tucker didn't know and didn't care that it was designed as a water hazard for the golf course. He gladly took a good long drink. The water tasted so good! Looking up, he saw a duck waddling near-by, and lunged to capture it. The duck hopped and fluttered across the water splashing along the way, landing on the other side of the pond.

He lifted his head to another noise. In the distance, he saw a golf cart headed his way at full speed. Curious, he stood watching until it pulled to a stop 10 feet away. A gray-haired plump, man with a big round tummy, jumped up, waving a rake and yelling. "Shoo, get away! What are you? A wolf? Get away!" The man grabbed some rocks and threw them at the white dog.

Tucker was startled, his tail dropped, and his head hung low as he turned and ran for the nearest cover, a hedge of bushes. He ducked under the bushes and sank on the cool dirt. The pot-bellied man, no longer able to see the dog, eventually turned and walked back to his cart. Tucker watched the frightening potbellied man crawl back on his cart and roll away. Tucker's tummy growled and he sat there silently for a while, not moving trying to decide if it was safe to look for food.

As the frightened animal lay there, he noticed so many birds along the golf course. There were finches, grackles, doves, quail, crow.

He calmed down as instinct drove him to focus on the little creatures, preparing to pounce and capture one. He waited silently, studying their every move. In the meantime, the flies and gnats found him hiding under the bush.

"Ahh," as he snapped at one. "I'll catch you!" He continued to snap at the flies until he caught one. He learned to wait motionless until one buzzed close to his eyes. Suddenly he snapped and caught the fly. It became a good game requiring little energy; and the tiny bites felt good in his empty stomach.

It didn't take long for him to discover more bugs living in the dirt, tiny round bugs, and beetles. He hopped up and began digging with energy, dirt flying around him. He found all kinds of bugs in the dirt. He learned to spend his time under the bush digging in the cool wet dirt looking for bugs, and waiting for bugs come to him.

Most of the time, his long white nose was black with dirt.

He continued to lie in the shade of the bush for several days, digging for bugs that were quite tasty on an empty stomach.

One evening, he heard rustling a few feet away, and he silently turned his head toward the noise. The leaves moved, and he automatically pounced. Out darted a ground squirrel and dashed away. Missed! He longed for another drink of water, but he was frightened of that potbellied man on the golf cart. He chose to follow the scent of water coming from a different direction. It was further away. A house, bordering the golf course, three doors down, was sprinkling its lawn. Realizing he would need to leave the safety of the bushes; he decided the risk was necessary. Slowly and quietly, he rose and walked toward the water. A puddle formed at the edge of the lawn, and he casually walked over for a taste. Tucker took a few laps spotting some bugs nearby. Snatching a couple, he found they were nice and crunchy. Bugs always helped ease the hunger pang in his tummy, but they never satisfied him. He continued to wander along grassy area which took him between two homes, and he approached a sidewalk.

"Mommy! There's a big dog over there!" Tucker looked up toward a voice past the house along its side yard. On the sidewalk, a young girl pointed at him. In a moment, a woman stepped from behind a tall green bush at the corner of her yard and looked at him.

The mother gasped and whispered as she grabbed the little girl, "It's a stray, honey! It looks scary. Let's go inside." As she turned, she saw a neighbor in his front yard and yelled, "Hey Steve, don't go over there! There's a loose dog coming this way."

Curious, the man walked towards the mother and child to see. "Oh, I see." The man said, "He's beautiful!" the man watched Tucker. The dog did not move when he saw the man. He tried to decide if this man was as dangerous as the plump potbellied man. Tucker thought about running.

The man took a step forward, "Come here pup! I won't hurt you." Tucker took a step sideways as he watched the man begin to walk his way. He braced himself to run. When the man saw the dog shift, he picked up his pace and hollered. "Wait!" and started running towards Tucker. The lonely dog did not know what 'wait' meant. But it reminded him of the man on the golf course.

The mother pulled her daughter back inside the house. The little girl protested as she wanted to see what would happen, but her mother knew it was best to go inside. The man kept walking towards Tucker. The dog braced his legs ready to run.

Alarmed, Tucker decided to run full tilt along the golf course toward the trees in the distance, leaving the man on the sidewalk, far behind him. Tucker loved the chase and ran with his tail high in the air. It curled and fanned behind him as he ran. Once in the trees, Tucker paused and turned to see if the man was following him. He didn't see anyone and decided to lie down in the trees thankful for the cool shade. He was far away from the pond now, and he wondered if there would be many birds, bugs and squirrels in these trees.

The thought of food made his stomach growl again. A fly flew by, and he snapped at it. Several more buzzed his head, and he caught one. He hadn't eaten anything but a few bugs for days. He lay still, and soon saw birds land in the branches overhead. He longingly gazed at the birds. Soon a covey of quail came dashing by a few yards away. Remembering the slow ones, he considered his strategy. In a silent lunge, Tucker leaped toward the quail and captured one of the last ones trying to run by. Tucker gently held onto it until he was back in the trees. It wasn't the same as dog food, but this bird did help the pain in his tummy settle down.

Chapter 4

Another Lonely Pup

Late one afternoon, Tucker lay under the bushes waiting for night fall. Afternoon was normally his nap time, but he heard and smelled something new. It smelled like a dog. Without moving his head, he opened his eyes to see what it was and there just in front of him was a little chihuahua. "That looks like Frisky!" Tucker thought, and he immediately thought of Robert and Karen. Tucker lifted his head and continued to lay there. The chihuahua slowly approached and reached out his nose sniffing Tucker. Tucker did the same. Encouraged, the chihuahua walked around behind the big white dog and continued to sniff Tucker. Tucker just lay there. Soon it was the big boy's turn to smell the little puppy.

The two began wagging their tails. Both were happy to be making a new friend. The chihuahua lay down beside Tucker in the shade of the bushes and the two took a nap together. As the sun went down, Tucker stood up to find water and the chihuahua followed. The pond was quite a distance by now, but most of the humans had gone for the day and Tucker felt it was safe. He had learned to hide in the shade of bushes and trees during the heat of the day, and search for food and water in the cool of the night.

Another night provided lullabies: owls hooting, coyotes howling, and ringtails rustling. They stayed under those trees for several days. The chihuahua shivered with the sounds and Tucker stood over him showing the little pup that he would be protected. This was a good thing because those owls would have enjoyed the tiny puppy for dinner.

One evening as night began to fall, they lay quietly under the bush, and Tucker heard a barely audible sound sliding on the gravel about two feet away next to a block wall. Its smell was intriguing. Tucker turned his head toward the sound without moving his body and saw a giant black and white snake slithering along the wall.

With his eyes glued to the snake, Tucker lunged in a flash. Landing on the snake, he caught it with his mouth and shook his head. The snake flopped helplessly back and forth.

The chihuahua, startled, stood, and backed away to watch Tucker swing the snake back and forth. The little puppy's eyes were wide open with astonishment. "What on earth is that?" The two dogs sniffed the dead snake for quite a while before attempting to take a bite. Tucker lay down with his prize, and the chihuahua sat about a foot away watching. Hunger finally gave the chihuahua courage to come forward to taste the snake. Tucker ignored the little dog as he continued to lick and smell the snake. The chihuahua took the first bite. It was tasty for a hungry dog and the little one began eating the snake. Tucker watched and soon followed suit.

Now, this was a fine meal! Tucker and the chihuahua settled down and slowly picked away at opposite ends of the dead snake, grateful for something in their tummies.

The two did not find anything substantial to eat for days after the snake. Tucker showed the little pup how to dig in the dirt for bugs. As tiny as the chihuahua was, those bugs were a perfect size for its tummy. However, in the time spent under the bushes, hungry blood-sucking ticks found Tucker. The chihuahua spent much of its time under the big dog, so the ticks kept landing on Tucker. The round flat bugs would drop onto him from the branches above, crawl around for a warm, safe spot out of Tucker's reach. There, they swelled up before dropping off. They were usually out of Tucker's reach, and there was little the stray dog could do.

Two days later, as the morning light began to break on the horizon, the two dogs headed toward their shady hiding spot under the trees. Suddenly Tucker stopped and stared ahead. The chihuahua kept walking toward their home under the trees. Tucker growled a warning and the chihuahua stopped to look back at Tucker. The large dog came up to the little pup and stood over him. With legs braced and head down, the dog hovered over the chihuahua and growled. The little one knew to stand still, completely bewildered, but it understood Tucker's warnings. Soon the chihuahua saw movement in the distance. It was a dog. Or it looked like a dog. But it was different and seemed dangerous! Neither of these lost dogs knew what a coyote was, but that is what they were watching.

The coyote was looking for breakfast and truly enjoyed the creatures that lived along the golf course. The coyote hoped to find something before the humans started arriving. The coyote stopped to study the two dogs and thought the little chihuahua was interesting, but the big one looked like it would be too much trouble to get to the little one.

Tucker growled quietly, warning the chihuahua not to move. Head down, he growled again and took a step toward the coyote. This move threatened the coyote, who looked away to show disinterest. It stood a little longer before turning away from the two dogs and trotted off.

Tucker relaxed his muscles but kept his eyes on the coyote. He did not want the wild animal to know where they slept, so he stood there a while longer. Then the coyote disappeared into the distance, Tucker realized they had to hurry to get out of sight before humans, like potbellied man, start arriving.

One evening the two dogs smelled something marvelous. Both remembered the smell of dog pellets, real food. Intrigued by the scent, the two got out from under the shelter of the bushes and walked toward a wire kennel set up near the golf course pond. As they neared the cage, the chihuahua ran toward it. They didn't know this, but it was a humane dog trap set out for Tucker. Tucker trotted along, staying close to the little dog. He was becoming quite protective of the little dog and wanted to be sure it was safe. The large dog had never seen anything like this, and being more cautious, hesitated at the door of the cage. But the chihuahua was familiar with kennels, was not afraid of the cage at all, and darted right in before Tucker could stop him, and headed directly for the dog food.

Then, clang! The door to the cage fell, and the chihuahua was caught. Startled, the chihuahua turned around and whined, but the food was enticing, and it easily distracted the little puppy. It turned back to the food and began eating. Tucker lay down and watched the chihuahua eat, envious. The big dog decided that maybe a drink of water would help the hunger pangs, so he got up for a drink at the pond. On his way, he noticed two women walking toward them. Alarmed, Tucker turned and ran away from the cage and the two humans. He slid under some bushes, lay down, and didn't move as he watched from a distance.

The two humans slowly walked up to the cage. "Well, hello there little one!" said one woman in a friendly voice. "We are looking for a big white dog, but it looks like you need help too!" The chihuahua was unusually friendly, whined a happy sound, and wiggled a greeting with its tail. A second woman sat down next to the chihuahua and let the dog smell her through the wires. She had spread a dabble of soft dog food on her hand, which the chihuahua licked.

Slowly they made friends, and the two women decided it was safe to open the kennel. The second woman gently lifted the chihuahua, saying, "Oh you are a sweet friendly thing! We will look for your people but if we can't find them, we will easily find a good home for you!" The chihuahua licked the woman's cheek as the woman laughed and turned her face away from the dog.

"Actually, Fran," the other said, "There was a lost chihuahua post just last week on the neighborhood feed! I wonder if this is their puppy." She went on, "It's so friendly. This guy is dirty and hungry, but it looks like he hasn't been on his own for too long."

"It's dangerous for little ones like you out here!" the first woman said as she held the chihuahua close. "If you've been out here a week, how did you survive?"

The other woman was packing up the cage. "Let's see if this is their puppy. I love it when we can get them home so quickly. This little one is lucky. He could have been a good meal for the owls and coyotes out there."

The woman holding the chihuahua nodded and smiled at the little pup, who was shivering with excitement. "What do you think, should we find another spot for this cage? I sure would like to find that husky-shepherd."

"Yes, first, let's check to see if we have had another sighting. We may need to move the cage again."

Before leaving with the chihuahua, the two women looked around, hoping to see the big white dog, but they couldn't see it. "I am sorry we didn't catch him," the first woman said. "But we will keep trying."

Tucker didn't move as he watched the women carry the little chihuahua away. He knew he wouldn't see that little dog again. It had been good to have a companion; now he felt lonely again. Tucker crawled out from the bushes and headed back to where the two dogs had slept the day before. It was time to get out of sight and into the shade. By now, Tucker was quite familiar with the grounds of the golf course and knew his way.

But the heavy man on the golf cart was watching for him and had figured out Tucker's hiding tricks.

Chapter 5

The Big Cave

It took a few days before the pot-bellied man found current Tucker's hiding place at the far end of the golf course. The shepherd-husky lay silently under the bushes hoping not to be noticed. As the man drove by, he stared into the bushes. "You, again! I knew I'd find you." the man hollered. He got off his cart, waving his arms and yelling as loud as he could, "Shoo! Shoo!" Alarmed, the stray got up and ran toward the houses away from the golf course.

When the man was out of sight, Tucker began looking for a new place to hide. Finally, he found a crawl space under one of the larger homes along the street. He liked the shade and shelter under the porch, but it didn't last long. The following evening, the homeowners let their dog out the front door. Following his nose, the dog smelled something strange under the porch. He discovered Tucker. The dog sounded an alarm by growling and barking, bringing humans to investigate. Concerned for their dog's safety, they grabbed their pet's collar and put a leash on him to protect it from whatever they might find under the porch.

The dog's master pulled back on his pet, fearing an attack by a wild animal. Tucker slid back to the darkest part of the porch, waited, and listened until the master dragged his dog back into the house. Tucker knew that meant they were all inside, so he crawled out from under the porch and took off running down the sidewalk.

The owner came back out to investigate. He was hesitant to look under the porch but came out armed with a flashlight and a broomstick. Thinking it was rats, he prepared to scare off whatever it was hiding under the porch. He started peering under the porch, banging the broomstick, and swinging the light back and forth. The man heard nothing. He looked up in frustration and saw a large white animal trotting down the sidewalk in the distance. Realizing the white animal had quietly slipped out the other end of the porch, the man squinted at the animal with curiosity. "Was that a wolf?" He paused then hollered as he ran back to the house, "Elizabeth! I think it was a wolf!"

Now, Tucker needed to find another hiding place. The smell of water attracted him, and he followed the scent leading him to a lawn sprinkler. Thirsty, the dog paused to lap from a small puddle along the edge of the yard. The noise of the sprinkler camouflaged the sound of footsteps of a hiker as he came by. "Hey there pup! What are you doing here?" the man asked. The man started slowly walking toward the stray, but the dog was still frightened of humans. The shepherd-husky started walking away from the stranger, and as the man began to run, the frightened dog ran full speed.

"Wait!" The man hollered, "I won't hurt you!" Tucker looked at the man running and yelling at him. This confused and frightened the dog, who turned his back to the man and moved away as fast as he could. As the dog rounded the block, he found himself on the sidewalk, going past rows of houses. The stray knew it was time to find a place to hide quickly, and tucked himself behind thick bushes along the shady side of a someone's home. The dirt was soft and cool, and he was content, except for the hunger. It had been three weeks now, and he was beginning to feel weak.

For days, he wandered and eventually came near a busy street with humans hiking along the same road. They waved their arms, yelling at him to get away from the street. In their efforts to protect him from fast-moving cars, the stray even became more frightened of humans. Finally, he turned away from the humans, turning his ears back to hear if they followed. Thankfully, he ran away from the busy street, trotting down the sidewalk and crossing some quiet side streets. The humans did not follow.

His priority now was to constantly follow the scent of water. He kept close to the grass along the golf course greens. But he kept moving as he tried to avoid people. That effort eventually led him away from the golf course, and the smell of the moist grasses of the golf course faded away.

When dark fell, he continued to listen to the rustle of the ringtails as they roamed in the night, paying attention to the direction they came from and where they went. He noticed the sounds always had the same pattern. They came from the golf course with the ponds and headed down a dry wash. He figured they were looking for food during the night, so he decided to follow their pattern and headed down toward the wash. Each night they lured him further away from the golf course. Finally, he came to the wash, which continued to lead him away from the golf course. The ditch was used to catch rainwater during a storm, but now it was dry and brittle with dead grass. Bushes and trees lined either side of the wash. He anticipated lots of birds, snakes, and other edible things living there. As he followed the wash, he came up to another busy street. Cars were dashing by. Despite the humans' efforts made a few days ago, Tucker had not yet learned about cars.

However, he instinctively knew to avoid the huge things whishing past so fast. But he was determined to get to the other side of the road. He waited for a quiet moment and leaped into the street. As he dashed across the street, a car pulled to a stop, and the driver watched him dash down the wash. The woman in the car pulled out her phone and made a phone call. "I just saw that shepherd-husky mix. He's headed down the wash toward the church!" Her husband was on the other line.

"Thanks, honey. At least we have an idea where the dog is! I will call the rescue team and let them know. Maybe they can set a trap for him."

Meanwhile, the stray trotted down the wash, not knowing what the future would bring.

Each night he ate bugs and hoped for a bird or snake. He lapped water from water sprinklers, but there weren't any along the wash. He needed to find homes with grassy yards. Finally, after some searching, he found where he could push through the bushes and slip into someone's yard to get to their water sprinklers. It was cool fresh water and tasted so good. It was the only house around that had water. He remembered, from the pot-bellied man, never to stay in the same place more than one night, so even though it might have felt like a perfect spot to wait, he knew he needed to move on.

As he wandered further down the wash, the grass and weeds became more brittle and bushes less plush. Homes were no longer behind the bushes. In the morning, he waited on the east side to stay in the shade. As the sun went down, he crossed the wash to the west side for shade. Water was more and more scarce.

One morning, he noticed another wire cage with some fabulous smelling food inside. He sat shyly and watched it from behind the bushes and noticed an unleased dog walking with his master along the top of the wash. The dog saw the cage and ran to it, dashing inside without hesitation. With a loud clang, a wire door fell behind him. This dog had never been in a kennel and squealed in panic as he jumped around inside the cage. He leaped from side to side as the wire box continued to rattle. The young shepherd-husky stray was alarmed as he listened and watched. The caged dog spun in circles, leaving the food untouched. The dog's owner came running to him. "Barney, what are you doing?" He bent over the wire box and opened it. The man paused, inspecting the cage, "What is this doing here? It's dangerous." He left the cage door closed and walked away. That night he asked about the cage through neighborhood online news.

"I found a cage at the wash near the church. Unfortunately, my dog got trapped in it. Does anyone know what that's all about?"

"There has been a stray husky-shepherd wandering around the golf course, and someone saw it head down the wash. They are trying to catch it."

"It's been wandering the area almost a month now!"

Local volunteer animal rescue folks had been trying to capture the dog for nearly two months. For some reason he kept evading the experts. They didn't know the stray was a such quick learner, who spent much of his time watching and observing everything around him. He knew to stay away from the cages by now, and it took only a few experiences to frighten him away from humans. He knew now, he would never go near a cage like that. He did not want to get stuck in one of those; and he knew Robert would not come to help him out! "No cages and no pot-bellied men!"

In the meantime, curious, about those nocturnal ringtails. The things he could hear but couldn't see. He was sure they were headed for food in their nightly travels. So, he continued to follow the sound of the ringtails.

Chapter 6

The Church

After seeing the dog get captured in the cage, Tucker decided to keep moving. The dry grass was tall and easy to hide in. But it was brittle and sticky. Not near as pleasant as the moist green grass of the golf course. He noticed the green grass was gone, but there were mice, squirrels, and birds living in and around those trees. So, he slowly worked his way down the wash. This area seemed to be where the ringtails come and go at night. By the sound of the ringtails, they traveled through the wash each night, and it might be a place to settle for a few days.

At dusk he lay in wait as the birds settled in the trees overhead. He hoped one would somehow land close enough for him to catch it. This technique never seemed to work. As the sun went down, darkness set in.

In the silence of the night, he listened for the quiet rustling of the ringtails, sniffing for mice and rats. He was thankful the air was not as hot as darkness of the night arrived.

By now, his energy was fading. He just was not up to running, hunting, and chasing for food anymore. So, he spent more time lying in cover waiting for bugs and unsuspecting mice to wander past him. The hot asphalt and rocks were beginning to burn the pads of his paws, leaving sores, so while he lay in wait for the bugs, he licked the sores. His pads had started to bleed, and dirt caked on the sores, so the blood red wounds turned black with the dirt. Each night he licked the wounds, which caked over again when he stood up to walk.

Pain filled each step as the hot sidewalk burned deeper into his paws. The dirt entering the wounds helped buffer the heat. But it was more difficult walking across jagged edges of gravel and rocks. Pain spiraled up his legs as sharp edges cut into the wounds on his pads. Still, hunger and thirst haunted him, and he kept moving. Finally, he noticed a faint smell of water up the hill on the west side of the wash. Early, during the cool of the morning, he gathered his energy, slowly stood, and crept up the hill, looking for soft spots to set his paws. He limped noticeably more on his front left paw, the most painful of the four.

Walking toward the smell of water, he saw a big parking lot and a building. He lay in the distance before approaching. He didn't know, but it was a church. It was a dry, hot summer, and the church folks had begun leaving water out for the animals of the desert. By now, this white shepherd-husky stray had become an animal of the desert, and he smelled the water. Concerned by the people coming and going, he lay quietly waiting, hoping not to be seen. He lowered his head as someone turned, gazed his way, and pointed. However, the group did not yell or chase him. Instead, they stood, pointing at him and murmuring. Several went inside and came out with a large pitcher to refill the water bowl. Then folks went about their business. As the day went on, the people faded away and the white shepherd-husky watched that bowl. The afternoon sun continued to heat the asphalt; he couldn't wait any longer. The smell of water called him as he slowly walked across the hot asphalt to the bowl burning his paws with each step.

At the bowl, he took a large drink of warm water. So thirsty, he splashed water out of the bowl with each lap, losing precious liquid. He didn't notice.

He turned and slowly headed back to the bottom of the wash and planning to return the next day. That morning, again, he crept up the west slope of the wash, and lay in the distance watching for people. The water bowl was there, and another was next to it. He waited until afternoon and slowly came forward to drink. He walked over to the new bowl and found dog food. Amazed to discover pellets of tasty food he was remembered his old friend Robert. "Ah, where is Robert?" he thought. Then the pup recalled, the last time he saw Robert, his master was lying motionless on the ground. The dog took a few bites and gently ate some pellets. A door opened, startling the dog, and he looked up. There stood a woman. She didn't approach him, but the stray turned and slowly walked away. She stood still, calling gently, "Come here boy, its ok." Tempted by her gentle tone, he was too frightened to respond. But he did plan to come back the next day.

The following morning, he headed up the west bank of the ditch. As he reached the top, he saw the same lady pouring pellets into the new bowl and refilling the water bowl. At the same time, a car pulled into the church parking lot. As the driver got out of the car, he waved and shouted, "Hi Eleanor!" He began striding toward her as she straightened up from the water bowl to see who had arrived. The woman did not speak and looked worried as she put her finger to her mouth.

The man didn't notice and hollered, "How are you?"

Our stray puppy, startled once again, turned away and headed back to the wash. "Time to move on," he thought. Becoming weaker and weaker in the long hot days, he lay in the dirt and listened to the ringtails. Early the following morning, he followed the sounds mice and rats and traveled further along the ditch. He was curious as he heard new sounds from above. But he was losing energy and didn't have the energy to explore the sounds. They were whishing sounds whizzing past and fading away.

Eventually, he saw a car whiz by overhead. "Ah, that's what is making that sound." He thought. He saw a dark space below and a hint of light in the distance. It looked like a wonderful shelter for shade. He knew that dark shady area would be cool. From a human's perspective, it was a bridge, and those fast-moving objects (automobiles) were whizzing by above his head.

The smell of rats, mice, and birds lured him closer to the entry. He started hiding just inside the cave to be out of the sun's heat. He lay quietly, hoping to capture a critter as evening approached. Exhausted, he fell into a deep sleep. If edible creatures darted by, he missed the opportunity for a meal.

Each night the cave pulled him in deeper where the mice and rats were hiding. He found holes in the soft dirt under the bridge and was able to find plenty of bugs.

One positive thing about this spot, he didn't have any ticks dropping on him. The last of the ticks finally fell off, and he was free of them for a while. As the mice came out in the evening, he was able to surprise and capture two! That night he slept well with a full tummy. In the morning, thirst was driving him back to the church's water bowl. He ventured out of the cave and headed back up the wash.

This time a man hiking along the top bank of the wash saw him. The skinny dirty white husky-shepherd looked even more wolf-like than before. The man started yelling and throwing rocks at him to shoo him away from the church and nearby homes. Then, looking back toward the cave, he saw the light at the end of the tunnel, and our poor puppy ran into the darkness and through the tunnel coming out the other side.

Chapter 7

The Other Side

As he came out the other side of the cave, he saw more dry brittle bushes. The pain of hunger was fading, and he was thankful for that. However, he had gotten thin and very dirty. He continued past the shade of the bridge, believing he had to keep moving. His paws hurt, and he walked tenderly toward the only shade he could see under the tree ahead. He was more and more discouraged as he became weaker.

The dog had been on his own now for six weeks. He thought of Robert, and he quickly put that out of his head as fatigue reminded him to go lie down in the shade.

Days went by, and he survived by eating bugs and capturing an occasional quail. He found water by following the scent of water. The scent guided him around the block wall, and there he found water sprinklers making puddles in the grass.

One morning as he headed for water, he peeked around the corner of the block wall and saw a bunny, inches in front of him. Immediately his instinct kicked in and he pounced on the bunny. What a prize that was, much better than all those feathers on birds! He lay next to the wall carefully exploring his catch and had a fine breakfast.

He had several reasons to be thankful for bunnies. Not only were they a good meal, but he also learned from them to hide along the shady side of homes near the water sprinklers. As he followed their lead, he was closer to them and might be able to catch another meal. He continued his plan to hide during the heat of the day and wandered at night in search of food and water. This plan was good, but he had discovered the best time to hunt was at dusk and dawn. The rest of the night was spent wandering among the houses searching for the next place to hide. Even though this new plan was better than waiting in the wash, he was at greater risk of being chased by humans.

He was weaker now, unable to run anymore. The hot sidewalk burned his paws so much he didn't notice hunger pangs any longer. He avoided walking on rocky areas as the

jagged rocks cut into his wounds. Instead, he
preferred hot concrete sidewalks over rocks
as he hunted for shady grassy places to hide.
Unfortunately, the grassy areas were few and
far between, not at all like the golf course.
The clumps of shady trees and bushes were
less numerous now; this area mainly had
rocks, block walls, concrete, and cactus. The
days became more difficult, and he was
anxious being out on the street where he
could be seen so easily.

Continuing his search, the dog finally came
across a home with sprinklers with new grass
and bushes. Happily, he slid up beside the
house for shade and lay on the grass under a
few bushes to rest for the night. He was
learning now that he was around houses; he
needed to watch for humans walking out the
door as he stepped out from behind the side
of their homes. These homes reminded him
that he had lived in a house long ago with
Robert. The lonely dog longed for a home
and to be loved by someone.

Still, he was frightened of humans. Traveling in the early morning or late evening, the sidewalk was less hot and fewer humans crossed his path. He learned long ago how to hide and stay silent. But even in the early morning, humans would spot him and run after him. Local morning walkers discovered him one morning. Even though he turned from them and walked away, frightened hikers threw rocks at him. "Look out! It's a wolf! I think he has rabies!" The humans didn't realize the pup's unsteady walk was from sore paws and weakness.

The humans posted on their neighborhood chat, they had seen a wolf that looked like it had rabies, triggering another string of comments.

"We had to shoo off a white wolf! He was walking weird! I think it had rabies!"

"That's not a wolf. I've seen it. It is a stray dog. I think it's a husky."

"The poor dog is starving, that's not a wolf, I saw it the other day."

"It is a husky shepherd dog. We are trying to catch it humanely. I wonder how he crossed the street!? We've been using humane bait cages for nearly two months now. Please let us know where you saw him, and if you see him again. We will set another one up tonight near your area."

That evening he saw two women set up a wire cage with food inside. They looked around as they began to leave, hoping they might see him. "I'm not sure how much longer he can go." One of the women said. "It sounds like he is not doing well."

The second woman agreed, "If we don't find him soon, it may be too late. We need the neighborhood folks to help. Let's put another post on the newsfeed asking people to watch for him and let us know as soon as they see him." All the while, he was hiding under a bush tucked up against the shady side of someone's home. The women didn't see him watching them quietly from a distance.

Sadly, our stray saw what happens when you crawl inside those things; and he will not go near it.

That evening, he got up and moved on, away from the cage. As he moved, he walked along sidewalks and block walls inspecting various yards. One evening he came across a lizard. The dog froze with his eyes wide open. He had never seen one of these. It was a brave little thing and bounced up and down, trying to threaten the hungry stray puppy. Motionless, the dog waited. But he waited too long. Suddenly the lizard darted into a crack in the block wall and disappeared. Our hungry puppy lunged after the lizard and pressed his nose over the crack where the lizard disappeared. He sniffed hungrily at the gaps hoping to find it.

He continued to sniff and blow into the crack, hoping the lizard would scramble out. But it was long gone. The dog finally gave up and wearily moved on to the next house, looking for shade on the east side. This time he found moist dirt at the base of some bushes, which made a soft, cool bed. He sighed with fatigue and relief as he sank to the ground. His sleep was restless as he tried to listen for the melodies of the night telling him whether something edible might be nearby.

The following morning, he got up, looking for sprinklers. As he came upon a row of hedges, he saw a bird taking a drink as well. He pounced at the bird, but his reflexes were slow now, and the bird flew off. In his clumsy effort to catch the bird, our stray puppy had pushed his head into the bushes.

He missed the bird, but he bumped into a dead twig on the bush. He pulled his head out from the dry, brittle bush, and the twig had broken off the bush and was stuck on his forehead. With one end of the twig dangling in front of his eyes, the frustrated dog lay down to brush it off with his paws, but it just went in deeper.

Frightened, he felt an urgent need to keep moving on as the twig bounced in front of his eyes. He trotted along as best he could with his sore paws and a stick hanging from his forehead. In about an hour, the weight of the twig gradually pulled itself out, and it dropped to the ground. The dog stopped to sniff and investigate the item that caused pain in his forehead. Relieved, he looked up and gazed into the distance, wishing, and hoping for food, water, and a place to sleep. Every day, every night, this was his hope. But he was weaker and weaker; although he just wanted to sleep, he was still able to put in the effort to survive. Slowly, he moved on.

A few days later, early in the morning, he heard a new sound, kind of like a cluck. The wind drifted a smell his way that was similar to the birds he'd been hunting. He didn't know what they were, but he was smelling chickens at the corner house ahead. His stomach no longer felt pain, nor did he crave food anymore, but instinctively he followed the scent, sniffing into the morning breeze and following his nose.

This time when he stood up, he didn't stretch his legs, something he used to love. Stretching took too much energy. His movements were slow now as he wandered up a hill and stopped to hide and rest at the top of the hill. He couldn't travel far, growing weary very quickly. He was so tired now. Finding food was too much for him. He lay on the shady side of a house the rest of the day, waiting for evening to bring relief from the sun.

That evening he began to wander down the hill toward the smell of the chickens across the street. As he drew near, a large animal came from behind a row of homes across the road, 20 feet in front of him. He watched it leap up and land atop a block wall right at the source of that smell! He'd never seen anything like it. This strange creature was a bobcat following the same scent he was following. Looking for dinner, the bobcat was just moments ahead of our stray puppy.

The chickens, however, were safely tucked inside a coop, and no predator would be able to catch them. Not wanting to attract the cat's attention, the weak shepherd-husky ducked beside a house as the bobcat jumped out of the chickens' yard and headed back the way it came.

After waiting a while, the dog decided to move on, looking for a good spot to rest. But as he walked past the chicken house, a young man saw him. Thankfully, a dog lover, the man guessed it looked like a husky. By the looks of the dog, he knew it was starving. He was on his way to work and couldn't do anything but take pictures and post it on the neighborhood news feed. As he walked around the dog taking photographs, the man could sense the dog's fear. He walked slowly around and never toward the dog. Anxious, our stray tried to gain some distance from the stranger. He quietly called to the dog, hoping he could make a connection, but the poor stray limped away as fast as his aching paws allowed; the sores had grown so deep. The starving dog's bones were showing, and he was covered with dirt, but the will to survive was still there and spurred him forward.

Chapter 8

A Friend?

Knowing he couldn't do more, the young man got in his car and left for work, planning to post his pictures on the neighborhood news feed. But it would have to wait until later. He had already delayed too long.

Our lonely stray continued moving forward, following the scent of water from the sprinklers up ahead and there, he found grass. Near the sprinklers, he came to a house that seemed unusually quiet. In fact, that home was vacant. It had sold, and the new owners were doing repairs before moving in. The dog headed up the walk to the dark, quiet front porch to rest for the night. He no longer spent his nights actively hunting. He had no more energy for hunting, and it was a perfect hiding place, if no humans came along. He fell deep asleep.

Around noon the next day, our puppy was still sleeping as several vehicles pulled up to unload materials in preparation for their project the following morning. Several men in white climbed out and began unloading big square blocks off their truck. By now, the nervous animal hadn't been near humans for a long time and decided to leave quickly and quietly. He weakly rose to his feet, tail sagging, and gently stepped out from behind the porch wall, submissively walking down the sidewalk as if he had somewhere to go. One of the men in white turned to see what was moving behind him and was surprised when he saw the dog. The man was not worried as the dog walked by; he saw it was weak and not dangerous.

Right about then, a woman from the house next door was pulling out of the driveway in her car. She noticed the dog walking down the sidewalk past the worker. Knowing the home was vacant, she stopped to ask the worker if it was his dog. "No," he said, "It just now came out from behind the porch wall. I didn't know it was there. Is it yours?"

"No," Kathy said as she stopped her car and got out to call the dog. The dog, weak and in pain, sped up to a trot to get away from her. The lady watched him continue down the walk. She saw him limp, tenderly, and slowly setting each paw down one at a time. The thin dog slowed down when she didn't yell or follow, and he stopped to turn and watch her. The stray saw her pull the car into the driveway and disappear into the house. He turned back and continued down the sidewalk, looking for another shady grassy spot to hide.

As she dashed into the house, she thought to herself, "This dog is in trouble." She packed a baggie of dog food and grabbed a leash. When she came back out, the dog was limping slowly on down the street. She hopped back in the car to catch up and tossed some food out to him. Oh, that food smelled so incredible, but our stray knew better than stop to eat. He tried valiantly to pick up his pace. Amazed that he didn't stop for the food, she followed the dog with her car and threw out dog pellets every few feet. It was so skinny; she knew the dog was starving. The desperate dog ignored the food, wishing it had time to take a bite, but it kept walking.

By now, the dog wasn't sure if he stopped now, whether he could he ever muster up the energy to start walking again. The woman realized following the dog with an automobile wasn't going to work, and that it was only scaring the starving animal. She decided to pull over and park her car.

Not saying a word, she got out and very slowly and casually followed from 20-yards away. She watched the dog turn up and walk across a grassy yard wet from the water sprinklers that had just finished watering.

The dog disappeared behind the side of the house. Now he was out of sight, but she was familiar with that spot and knew where he would be hiding. So, she figured it would be a good place to casually walk past him and pretend not to notice he was there. By ignoring him, she could get closer and sit down with the dog food pellets. As she walked by, she turned her head and, sure enough there was the dog.

There it lay in the shade, on the damp, cool ryegrass watching Kathy. Kathy thought, "It's a beautiful white dog, sitting there tall and proud."

Looking around, she considered her options. With a small baggie of dog food, she decided to sit on the block walk where it met the sidewalk, 15 feet away from the pup. With her back to the starving dog, she spread the pellets on the wall about 3 feet away from her body. She sat quietly with a leash in her lap, occasionally peeking to see what the dog was doing. Initially, the dog sat against the wall of the house, alert, gazing at her with its beautiful golden eyes, ears forward. After what seemed to be an hour, she looked and noticed the dog had crawled about eight feet toward her. She hadn't heard him move at all; he had been so quiet.

She looked away again, waiting. Kathy said nothing, waiting and listening for the dog. But the animal was so very quiet; she could hear nothing. The silent dog crawled carefully across the soft, tender rye inching closer to that scent of dog food. Our hungry puppy remembered Robert had something that smelled and looked like that. Those cages had food too, but this time there were no cages. Just plain simple food!

Kathy sat still with her back to the dog, peeking only briefly. Our stray hoped this woman wouldn't jump up and yell at him as the others had. She was silent and that encouraged the starving dog. Desperate, he crawled a little closer and lay his head on the block wall a few feet away from the food. Kathy slowly took her hand and lay it on the block wall and slid the food toward him. She left her hand there so he could smell her. He gently took a bite, "So good!" He tenderly ate a couple more bites.

Kathy laid some more pellets next to her side to encourage him to crawl closer to her. Finally, he felt safe with this woman and was more confident, so he crawled within arms-length of Kathy and ate the food tentatively. He took just a couple pellets at a time, chewing each bite carefully. The food felt funny in his empty stomach; it had been so long. But it did taste good. All he had the past few days was dirty water and grass.

She quietly watched him eat and knew he was a gentle animal by watching how carefully he ate.

Kathy laid the leash beside him. He knew what it was, and it reminded him of Robert. Kathy gently dropped it over his head. Tucker didn't move as she pet him. He laid his head down on the grass as if to show submission and his trust. She slid the leash closer to the dog's head as it continued looking away, showing his trust. She draped the leash gently on his neck, and he didn't move. He knew what a leash was, and it did not frighten him. Kathy smiled. "Someone has loved this dog." She thought. Slowly, she held her breath as she laced the loop over his head, and he was secure! She released her breath quietly with a long sigh of relief.

He continued to lie there motionless, thankful to find someone who was kind. Kathy gave him more pellets to reward his gentleness.

They sat there a little longer, and Kathy made a phone call to the local humane society, advising them she had a stray dog. The man explained they were swamped, and it might be an hour before they could come. Discouraged, she hung up, hoping it would be sooner than an hour. It had already been an hour since she sat down on the wall. In her hurry, she'd forgotten water, and the heat was getting uncomfortable. She looked around, thankful it was mid-afternoon, and hoped it would not get any hotter than it already was. Soon the shadows would grow long and ease the harshness of the heat.

She knew this dog could barely walk, and she didn't dare try to walk him back to her home. She began to pet him, and he continued to lay there quietly. He let her touch him, thankful for her gentle hands. Wondering how old he was, Kathy gradually pet his nose, lifted his jowls on one side, and saw bright white shiny new teeth. "Ah, a young guy you are!"

Then she asked., "Are you a boy or a girl?" as she pet his back and gently lifted his hind leg. "Ah, a boy!" She decided to look at his paws since he had so much trouble walking. She was stunned by the dirt-caked bloody paw pads. "Oh, fella, your pads must hurt so much! How long have you been on your own?" The two continued to wait in the hot afternoon. He was used to the heat by now and they were still in the shade at least. But Kathy began to feel sweat dripping down her forehead, taking off her glasses periodically to wipe them down.

As they sat, Kathy had time to think. Normally a busy woman, she found sitting with this dog was peaceful and relaxing. She thought to herself, "It's amazing how therapeutic an animal can be, even if you just sit next to each other." She began thinking ahead, "Now, how am I going to handle this? What is my husband going to say?" Her husband was returning that afternoon from an out-of-town trip. "He will be surprised to find this guy hanging around." Kathy considered her two little cavaliers at home. "They will be surprised too!" She was enjoying this quiet time with the gentle giant. Kathy had fostered and rescued dogs over the years and knew that new rescues must be quarantined until a vet has given them a health clearance to be around other dogs. So, she considered how to keep him separated from the others. The vet's office would be closing shortly, and Kathy hoped she could get him to their office to check for a microchip; just maybe, this poor pup could go straight home. He was such a gentle dog; she figured his owners must have been looking for him. But, on the other hand, considering what bad shape he was in, he had to have been on his own a long time. Hopefully, his owners didn't give up.

Eventually, neighbors noticed Kathy sitting there and knew it had been over an hour. They were concerned. The women from across the street, Emily and Patricia, knew Kathy. They were animal lovers too and were known on the block as the informal local cat rescue team. They could see a dog lying next to Kathy in the grass and decided to wait a bit longer not wanting to interfere. But after a few minutes, Kathy had not moved, so they came to check on their friend.

The dog didn't move as the two women approached. Then, discovering Kathy's dilemma, the women offered to bring water. Kathy and the dog were thankful for help.

"How long have you been here?" Emily asked.

"I've lost track, it's probably been a couple of hours. I just can't get him back to the house. It's too far, and he can't walk very well." Kathy responded, then she asked, "Did you see his paws?"

The women stepped up as Kathy held one of his paws and pointed to the bottom of his pads while the dog lay there, grateful for gentle attention. "Oh, that's painful!" They remarked upon seeing the mud-packed sores."

"I've called the humane society, and they said it would be an hour. That was almost two hours ago." And she added, "The guy sounded swamped."

"We will keep an eye on you. Call us if you need anything."

"Thank you so much." Kathy responded. "We will wait here a little while longer. Still worried, Emily and Patricia left. After a short while the women returned. "We have an idea! We can bring over a sheet, and together we can lift him into the back of our SUV, and we will drive you to your house!"

Kathy was relieved, "That would be great!" But she was worried, "I hope we can lift him." Then added, "I'm not sure if he will let us."

By now, it had been almost three hours. The women left and quickly brought out a bedsheet, the SUV, and their nephew for added lifting power. The four humans rolled the exhausted, starving shepherd-husky onto a sheet. He lay there, allowing the humans to move him. He was too weak to either help or protest. Then the humans, each one taking a corner of the sheet, lifted the limp dog into the back of the SUV. The dog briefly lifted his head to see where he was and lay it down again with a deep sigh.

As it happened, the SUV was facing away from Kathy's home. Rather than make a u-turn, Emily decided to back the car the full block length to Kathy's house. By then, there was chatter and laughter as Emily navigated in reverse. Kathy stayed in the back with the dog holding the leash with one hand and resting her other hand on his bony ribs. He was motionless. The four humans lifted him out of the SUV, carried him to the front porch. It was gated and surrounded by a three-foot wall. Thinking the weak animal was relatively secure, Kathy went in for more water, a blanket, and food, while the others stayed with him. But suddenly, he felt the need to leave and, he jumped from a lying position up and over the porch wall. Stunned by his unexpected leap, the startled neighbors were still able to catch his leash and hold on to him.

As Kathy came back out, she noticed he was no longer on the porch. Puzzled, she looked down where he had been. Emily, Patricia, and their nephew called out to her, "He's over here, he leaped over the wall," they said, "Just like that! But we have him!"

Looking over the wall, Kathy saw the dog lying quietly next to his new human friends. "Oh my gosh! He's a jumper!" Kathy responded as she stepped over to take the leash. "Thank you!" She watched as the dog looked down the street into the distance, his eyes a bit wild. "Maybe it was panic," she wondered; Kathy didn't know. His need to escape was strong. He wanted to hide, but his weakness left him without the power to move. He had put all he had into that jump over the wall and there was nothing left anymore. "I wonder if he's a runner. Is that how he ended up here? Did he run away from his owner?"

Kathy took his leash and slowly coaxed him back, realizing she would need to sit outside with him until her husband arrived. He wasn't due for another hour. The neighbors returned home, offering to be of help if Kathy needed it.

During that hour, Kathy had plenty of time to make plans for the next steps. Realizing animal control may not likely be able to help anymore that day, she hoped her husband would get home soon. She spoke to the stray, "The first thing you're gonna do, is visit the vet." She still hoped to find a chip.

It was nearing 5 P.M., so Kathy called her vet to explain her predicament. They assured her they could at least check for a chip yet that evening and that they would be there until 5:30 P.M. Kathy scheduled an appointment for a complete check-up for the following morning. She hung up and looked at the thin white dog, "Okay, we have a half an hour!".

Just ten minutes later, her husband drove up. Thrilled, she stood and waved at him from over the porch wall as he pulled up the driveway. Curious, he parked and walked toward her. "Strange," he thought, "Why would she stand there waving at me like that?" She looked down and pointed, hoping to prepare him for what he was about to see. Peering over the wall, he saw, lying at her feet, an emaciated white dog with golden eyes gazing at him, a water bowl at his side. Wide-eyed and speechless, Craig looked at Kathy, tilting his head as if to ask, "What?"

Speaking quietly and quickly, "Well......" and she told him her story. At the end of the story, she quickly added, "And honey, we need to rush him to the vet before they close. Hopefully, he is chipped. We have less than half an hour! Can you help me run him over to the vet to see if there is a chip? Then, maybe we can find its owner. "

Knowing his wife was committed to this plan, he sat down with the dog and said, "Ok, give them a call, tell them we are on the way." Again, the dog was lifted into the back of an SUV. Kathy crawled in beside him as

Craig drove to the nearby vet. As Craig backed up to the vet's door, Kathy called the office. The vet tech came out with the chip reader and looked at the puppy. There was no chip. They did a quick check of his teeth and looked at his bloody paws. "Those wounds are probably from the hot pavement." The tech explained, "And, look! His nails are so short. That's also from constantly walking on the asphalt."

Driving back home, Kathy tried to figure out where to keep him overnight. They did not have a kennel for this size dog. Craig had an office next to his workshop, where they could keep him separated from the other dogs. "Craig, I'll stay with him in the office tonight."

"No," Craig responded, "I will stay with him."

"But Craig, it's my fault we are in this predicament. You shouldn't have to do it."

Once they were home, she took him straight to the office while Craig brought food, water, and a dog bed where Kathy and the dog waited. Then, Craig brought Kathy dinner.

Kathy took a picture of him lying down and posted it on the neighborhood news feed.

"FOUND LARGE WHITE DOG! Looks like a white shepherd."

Responses exploded on the feed.

"Oh, is it a husky or German shepherd? Hard to tell from pics."

"Looks more like a shepherd than husky."

"Oh, thank you. I have been driving around looking for him."

"Ok. Thanks. I will sleep better tonight. It is not my dog, but I saw the posts about him. He has been roaming the area for a long

time. Don't send him to animal control yet. I will check the Husky Facebook group to see if they recognize him. Can you take him to a vet to see if he is chipped? If you need help, let me know. I am a dog lover."

"I did take this guy to the vet; he is not chipped. I will quarantine him. I took a stray in years ago, did not quarantine him, and every dog in the house ended up infected with kennel cough. Thank you so much for checking. Would love to find its owner. I was finally able to befriend him a block from my house."

"There is a group in the neighborhood trying to catch him. I will send you their number, they will help you find the owners."

"Call the neighborhood rescue group, they have been looking for a white stray. I sure hope it's him, but if not, thank you for helping the dog you have."

"Oh, she just called, a wonderful resource. Thank you! She told me he had been seen around down by the golf course. He covered plenty of ground. I am thankful I had a free afternoon, and it wasn't too hot outside. I think he just got so weak, he let me make friends. She will help us look for the owner. He is quarantined in our garage, (we have two dogs already). We are alternating backyard potty runs. He is deep asleep now."

After hearing all the effort made to capture this dog, Kathy considered how things fell into place leading to this moment. The dog was on the verge of giving up; he had no more energy. He was weak; his paws were sore; he couldn't run anymore. Then, he walked by her house on a day she happened to have the time to sit with him for four hours.

That night, the humane society called at 9 P.M., to check in on the found dog. The harried man apologized for the late hour but explained they had been busy all night. He knew it was too late to be of any help but wanted to follow up anyway. Kathy was exhausted and told them she had gotten the dog home and would keep the dog until they find his owner. She explained she had assistance from the local dog rescue group that will help post flyers locally on the street, in social media and on the neighborhood newsfeed. The worker seemed relieved as their facilities were overcrowded. "Thank you!" the worker said, "The dog will be better off with you!"

The two slept in the office for a restless night. The dog panted continuously. Kathy listened to his breathing as she tried to sleep; perhaps it was stress and hunger that caused him to pant so much.

Chapter 9

Becoming Cooper

The following morning, they took him to the vet. During the visit, the doctor explained the dog is probably about 18 months old. He estimated the dog may have been on its own for about two months. He explained the stray was very thin but was encouraged because he was just above the threshold for organ damage. The veterinarian felt the stray would be okay with rehabilitation. However, the doctor pointed out, the animal probably would not have lasted much longer without help. The veterinarian did not have any other health concerns, nor did the dog appear to have anything contagious. He gave the dog the standard immunizations, recommending they keep the dog separate from their other pets for a few more days to monitor his health and see how he adjusted to the home.

The two cavaliers were extremely curious and knew there was another animal in Craig's office, so the minute they had a chance, they scurried out the door and peered into the office door to investigate. When they saw an unfamiliar dog through the glass door, they began barking, creating much commotion.

The new dog was still very weak and tired. He lifted his head to see what the commotion was about and lay there watching through the window a few minutes. Once the weak dog realized the two cavaliers were not coming through, he relaxed. He had no energy to try and make friends with a pair of noisy dogs. With food in his tummy and a water bowl nearby, he rested. After about half a day, the cavaliers realized they would not be meeting this dog very soon, so they decided to go about their own business.

The neighborhood rescue group prepared a poster to help find this beautiful white dog's owners.

The neighborhood newsfeed continued.

"How is your husky-shepherd?"

"The vet believes he will be okay. Now, we are looking for its owners. We will foster him for now. He is such a nice dog; someone has to love him somewhere. We reached out to a local group that helps strays. They are going to help us find the owners."

"Thank you for the update. Yes, I know the group. That's good news. She tracked his sightings on a map. So glad he's a nice dog, healthy considering what he's been through. This just makes my day! I cannot thank you enough for helping him. You are wonderful and kind soul to foster him until he's healthy. Knowing he is safe brings tears to my eyes. Can I help you with anything?"

"Thanks, I'll let you know."

As Craig and Kathy ate dinner the next night, they considered recent events. Craig tried to imagine what it was like for this dog, "The vet thought the dog was about 18 months old, and based on the dog's paws and low weight, this dog could have been on his own for about two months." Craig went on, "That would have been two very hot months. We live in the desert. A terrible time of year to be lost from home."

The two considered the best time to introduce the dogs to each other. Kathy and Craig did not know how the big dog would respond to their little Cavaliers. But the two agreed, "It might be a good to do give it a try while he is still weak from his experience."

One evening late in the day, as the dogs were low on energy, Craig and Kathy let the weary shepherd-husky in the backyard. They started with one little dog at a time. Immediately the stray showed submission.

He lay on the ground and rolled on his side. He let the senior dogs know he recognized they owned the yard. The little dogs walked about the yard sniffing and wandering, ignoring the big-strange dog. In time, the shepherd-husky rolled entirely on his back as the little ones wandered close still pretending to ignore him. The white stray continued to lay on his back, waiting.

Slowly the little ones approached the new dog and began to sniff him. The shepherd lay quietly for a moment and then rolled over onto his stomach and began to sniff the little ones in turn. Craig and Kathy smiled, "This was going well!"

Soon the three were good friends. Each day the two little ones would hunt the yard for interesting smells showing the new dog the best places to inspect while the big boy would rest and watch.

In the meantime, the hunt for the stray's owners continued. Kathy kept in touch with the neighborhood rescue group as they posted 'Found Dog!' notices with images of the stray on social media sites, the neighborhood news feed, lost dog websites, and posters.

Several dog lovers offered to adopt him. But no one claimed him as theirs.

The dog was eating, gaining weight, and his paws were healing. Kathy brushed him frequently. His coat was thin, and very little hair came out in the brush. After washing the dirt off his paws, Kathy kept them clean, checking them daily to ensure they were healing. He continued to walk carefully, avoiding rock and rough terrain. The new animal seemed to prefer the grass and the block patio. But it was only a matter of days before he began to walk more confidently. She was surprised to see his paws heal so quickly. By the third day, he was almost walking normally.

As he gained energy, he began running and jumping like a puppy again! Craig brought out a doggie toy from the dogs' toy basket, and the new pup was thrilled. He loved running after the tossed toy. He captured the toy, threw it into the air and leaped for it, turning, and dashing back to Craig, giving it to the human for another toss.

Craig and Kathy were thrilled to see the new dog jumping and playing in the yard.

During quiet moments, Kathy and Craig noticed he would climb up behind the bushes and watch the rest of the family from a distance. The couple often ate on the patio, and the new dog always sat under the bushes watching the humans and the other two dogs.

Often, he stood in the yard gazing over the block wall fence, with his ears alert and tail high. "I keep worrying he's a jumper!" Kathy said. "Maybe that's how he ended up A stray." Kathy continued to observe the dog's behaviors, trying to get a clue of his history.

She couldn't understand how someone could let go of such a wonderful dog.

The dog discovered the dogs' toy basket and would gently pull a small-sized toy and carefully carry it to his quiet spot under the bushes. He would muzzle his new toys, but he never destroyed them. His favorite was an old 3-inch yellow rubber pig. He carried it around carefully squeaking it, but he never bit into it. Kathy found herself routinely going to his bush hideout, collecting toys, and returning them to the basket. Their new giant puppy would again take them, one at a time, back to his hiding spot.

Kathy and Craig tried hard not to get attached to their visitor. But the dog was intelligent, kind, polite, and gentle. It soon became apparent they would not be able to give him up. They loved the dog.

At bedtime, the whole family slept in the same room. One night when going to bed, the new dog jumped up on the bed. In a loud voice, Craig hollered, "Down!" The startled pup immediately jumped down and sat at Craig's feet, looking up obediently. The dog looked at Craig with deep admiration and respect. He waited patiently for direction. Craig praised him for obeying his command. And the dog wagged his tail, lay on the floor, and went to sleep. From then on, the stray was constantly at Craig's side.

Finally, Craig looked at Kathy and said, "If no one comes up as his owners, let's keep him." Kathy smiled quietly, thinking, "I'm so glad, I was hoping Craig would want him." Then she said aloud, "That works for me. I think this was meant to be, considering how everything fell into place."

Then the search for a name began. What do we call him?" They considered many names. Kathy wanted to be sure they had a name that they could easily call out so he would hear them and come back if he ran away.

"How about General?"

"No, a great name, but...."

"Captain? No, General is better for this guy."

"Cooper?"

Finally, at a loss, they settled on Cooper. "Cooper it is!"

Kathy and Craig had already begun training him. They soon found it wasn't necessary, and it became apparent right away, he already knew sit, stay, and come. The dog responded quickly to the commands, wagging his tail waiting for praise. He loved to make his master happy. The treats didn't matter. What he wanted was praise. "He's been well trained." Craig said. "Someone has loved this dog."

Then one evening after dinner, Craig was outside working with Cooper. "Kathy! Look at this!" Kathy was doing the dishes, standing at the kitchen window. Cooper was in the far corner of the yard, Craig faced Cooper and slowly raised his arm in the dog's direction. Cooper looked at Craig, suddenly alert and dashed to Craig. "Good dog, Cooper!" Craig pet Cooper vigorously. Cooper was thrilled to please his new master.

Kathy smiled, thinking, "Never thought we'd have a dog like this! He is a gift and such a joy to have. He and Craig have something special." Then she added, "Yes, someone has loved this dog."

Epilogue

"Cooper, come!" Standing in the kitchen, Craig held Cooper's pack and waited for his dog to come. Excited, the dog first dashed past Craig into the living room, spun around and returned to his master with his tongue hanging out and smiling. The dog sat waiting for Craig to put the backpack on his back. Craig filled the pack with water for them both, a water bowl, snacks, and poop bags. Cooper's job is to carry the pack.

Each morning Cooper goes through the same ritual as he prepares to go on their morning hikes. He loves the desert now that he has a master and a home. Craig loves bringing his best friend along on these daily hikes. They are so much more enjoyable now. During one of their hikes, Cooper surprised Craig as they walked by a shrub along the trail.

Cooper suddenly jumped into the shrub as they walked by, and he caught a mouse.

Stunned, Craig looked down. "How did that happen?" He thought, "We were just walking by." For Cooper, it was a reaction triggered from memory. Things he had to do to survive. The difference now is that Cooper was strong, healthy and his responses are quick and accurate. Proudly Cooper let the mouse go, he didn't need it anymore.

Occasionally Cooper becomes alert, staring into the distance. The first time it happened, he stared just north of the trail toward the preserve's mountain. Craig stopped trying to see what Cooper was watching. Cooper didn't move. Neither did Craig. Craig's eyes searched the mountainside, seeing nothing. Then, he looked down briefly at the Cooper to see where the dog's eyes were pointing. Following the direction of the dog's gaze, Craig saw it. About 400 yards up the hill, there was movement. As Craig watched, he could see a coyote trotting along parallel to their trail. It blended well into the vegetation of the mountainside. "How did Cooper spot

it?" Craig wondered. The two hikers stood and watched the coyote trot along slowly, heading further from them. Cooper didn't need to lower his head or growl this time. The coyote was no threat.

During their hikes, Cooper is not interested in drinking water or having a snack. Usually, at the halfway point, Craig offers him a drink. But the dog is continuously on alert. He will sniff the water, then look back to the mountains, watching, listening, and smelling. He does not want any distraction from his job protecting his master and his home. He is too busy to take a drink. However, upon arriving home, Craig unleashes Cooper as they enter the yard, and the dog dashes in the house through the doggie door, heading straight for his water bowl. It is empty within minutes, splashing water all around the bowl, Cooper doesn't care.

It should be noted, immediately after they decided to keep the dog and gave him a name, Craig replaced the small doggie door with a larger one Cooper could use. Now, the loyal husky-shepherd can follow his master in and out of the house, everywhere he goes. Whether they are our back in the shop, off to Home Depo, to get gas, to the carwash, Cooper is beside Craig.

Cooper's Story

Cooper's Story

About the Author

Holly Bohling has a master's degree in Communication and is retired from an entrepreneurial career in program and business development serving people with disabilities, aging, and mental health. She has published and received awards for technical and research papers, however; her latent passion has always been her love for storytelling based on life experiences, history, and family lore.

Bohling grew up with pets, cats, bunnies, dogs, and even had a pet skunk for a while; and spent many hours with her pets. As an adult, she has fostered dogs, rescued and adopted strays, and purchased dogs from quality breeders. She loved each of them for the gifts they brought to her life.

Bohling imagines stories about life as she observes events evolving around her, including her experience with animals. Mysteries are particularly intriguing for Bohling. Homeless pets trigger her vivid imagination as she creates stories about their history. Filling the unknown gaps with her creativity, she gathers available facts and observes the dog's behavior to keep her stories realistic. Bohling weaves a narrative of what life might have been like for her rescue pets before they were found and placed in a good home. Bohling describes the feeling of a story forming in her head to be much like a song going over and over in her head. These stories replay in her mind until she finally writes them down.

Acknowledgements

A special thank you to my grandchildren, for their support and enthusiasm as I wrote this story. Their advice was helpful throughout the writing of this book. They are my greatest fans, and both love animals, especially dogs, with the same passion as mine.

Thank you to my husband for his patience, the time he gave to review my work, and his honest feedback. Another thank you to James K. Fruehling for suggesting I write this book. The process has been a joy.

I'd like to send out a huge and heartfelt thank you to all the rescue workers. The list is endless, from your neighbor who steps out to help an animal in distress, to rescue and foster workers who provide care for found pets, providing homes until they find a permanent place to live.

In addition to the rescue workers, a special thanks to the incredible people that adopt foster pets, giving them forever homes.

On the other end of the spectrum, a shout of appreciation to our quality breeders, who work hard to assure their puppies are strong and healthy. These breeders incur great expense to find the healthiest animals to breed future generations and work hard to eliminate genetic impurities that cause suffering and pain for our pets. In addition, they are careful to place their puppies in responsible, loving homes. They match their puppies with the new owners based on energy and personality. And just as important, they require new pet owners to return their new puppy if they cannot keep the dog for any reason, to assure the puppies they bring into this world are always well cared for and safe.

Another group of animal lovers must be recognized, our veterinarians, veterinary technicians, assistants, and those that clean the kennels. These people respond quickly and efficiently to animal emergencies, dealing with panicked pet owners, and patients that cannot verbally describe what is happening to them. Diagnosis and developing a plan of care is often a challenge.

I admire the hard work and expense these animal lovers incur as they carry out their calling to help our best friend and am humbled and grateful and honored to be a part of this amazing community of animal lovers. Because of them, Cooper has a story to share.

End Notes

40 Pets by the Numbers: 40 Pet Statistics for 2021

https://petpedia.co/pet-statistics/ 6.14.2021

- Around 1 in 10 people are allergic to pets.
- There are around 5,000 tigers kept as pets in the United States.
- Elderly pet owners make 30% fewer visits to their medical practitioners than those who do not have pets.
- Around 44% of people would rather cuddle up with their pet than with their life partner.
- According to pet statistics, owning a dog may decrease the risk of heart disease-related death by 36%.
- There are more than 200 million stray dogs in the world.
- It's estimated that around 1.5 million animals are euthanized in shelters every year.

- In 2019, around 2% of healthy or adoptable dogs and cats were euthanized in Canadian shelters.
- Americans spent around $99 billion on their pets in 2020.
- Online pet food sales rose by 77% during the March, 2020 Coronavirus lockdown.

[ii] **Animal Rescue Workers**

https://pictures-of-cats.org/animal-rescue-workers-have-the-highest-suicide-rate-among-american-workers.html
6.14.2021

[iii] **Compassion Fatigue**

https://barkpost.com/good/compassion-fatigue-animal-workers/   6.14.2021 https://pictures-of-cats.org/animal-rescue-workers-have-the-highest-suicide-rate-among-american-workers.html   6.14.2021

https://www.psychologytoday.com/us/blog/animal-emotions/201701/empathy-burnout-and-compassion-fatigue-among-animal-rescuers   6.18.2021

www.ingramcontent.com/pod-product-compliance
Lightning Source LLC
Chambersburg PA
CBHW060352180626
46817CB00008B/2975